# My Amazing Collection of Magical Stories

This igloo book belongs to:

.......................................................

# igloobooks

Published in 2023
First published in the UK by Igloo Books Ltd
An imprint of Igloo Books Ltd
Cottage Farm, NN6 0BJ, UK
Owned by Bonnier Books
Sveavägen 56, Stockholm, Sweden
www.igloobooks.com

0823 005
2 4 6 8 10 9 7 5 3
ISBN 978-1-80022-450-6

Written by Stephanie Moss
Illustrated by Antonella Fant

Designed by Bethany Dowling
Edited by Claire Mowat

Printed and manufactured in China

# Contents

igloobooks

# Fairysaur Surprise

It was Flyss the fairysaur's birthday. That night, there was going to be the biggest party Fairyland had ever seen so all the fairies could celebrate with her. The only problem was, none of them could think of a present to get Flyss, and they were starting to panic.

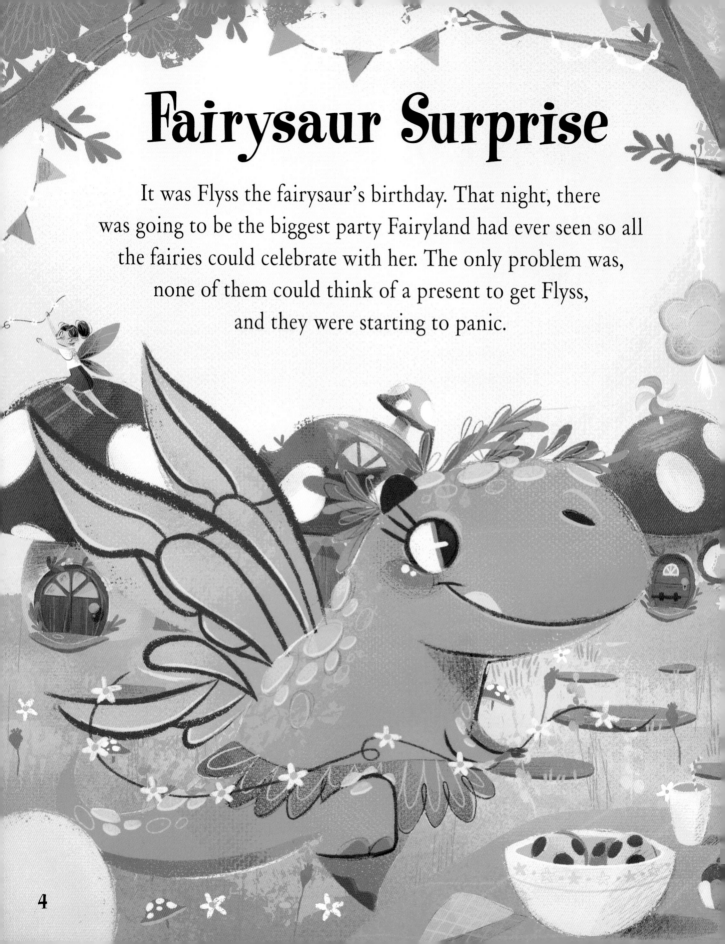

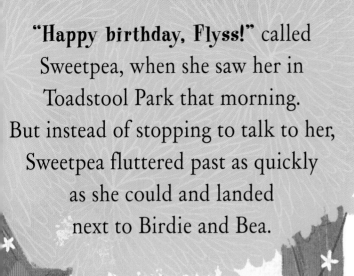

"Happy birthday, Flyss!" called Sweetpea, when she saw her in Toadstool Park that morning. But instead of stopping to talk to her, Sweetpea fluttered past as quickly as she could and landed next to Birdie and Bea.

"Where are we going to find a fairysaur-sized gift in Fairyland?" whispered Sweetpea.

5

Her friends shrugged. **"I don't know,"** replied Bea.
**"I've been worrying about it all week!"**
When Flyss wasn't looking, the fairies
hurried into Mr Bowtie's Boutique.

Mr Bowtie's Boutique

**"It's our friend the fairysaur's birthday,"** said Birdie.
**"Please, can you help us?"** So, Mr Bowtie disappeared into a
storage cupboard and rustled and rummaged around.

When he came back, he was carrying a huge
pile of clothes. **"How about these?"** he asked.

There were beautiful sequined
ballgowns that trailed along the ground
and full-length skirts with frills and bows,
but nothing that would fit a fairysaur!

Next, they tried Miss Sparkle's jewellery shop. They were sure there would be something beautiful they could get Flyss for her birthday. **"We've got the finest emeralds and diamonds from the deepest dragon mines, and pearls from Mermaid Cove,"** said Miss Sparkle.

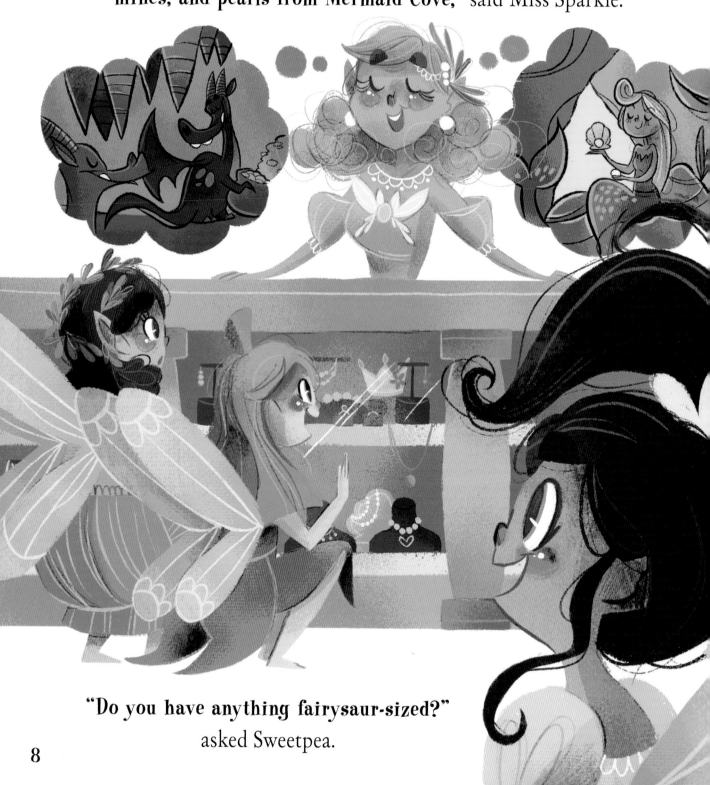

**"Do you have anything fairysaur-sized?"** asked Sweetpea.

Miss Sparkle looked nervous and then she disappeared, just like Mr Bowtie had. When she returned, she showed Sweetpea a **sparkling** tiara, helped Bea try on **twelve** different coloured rings and put a **long** gold necklace around Birdie's neck as she twirled in front of the mirror.

But a fairy-sized necklace wouldn't fit a fairysaur.

Finally, they visited Mr Frosting's Bakery. He was famous for baking the biggest cakes in all of Fairyland, and Sweetpea stared up at all the **delicious** treats that towered high above them.

"If we can't find a present," she whispered, "at least we can get Flyss the best cake ever."

The fairies spent the whole afternoon tasting **gooey** chocolate cakes, bubblegum pies and marshmallow whirls until they couldn't eat another bite. But then they thought about Flyss.

**"Even this triple-layered, caramel-crusted, strawberry drizzle sprinkle surprise would be like a tiny cupcake to our favourite fairysaur,"** said Bea.

On the way to the party, Flyss's friends were nearly ready to give up.
But then, when the stars came out and began to **twinkle**, Sweetpea had an idea.

With a swish of her wand, huge bursts and flashes
of colour lit up the whole night sky.

"HAPPY BIRTHDAY!" she called when Flyss arrived,
and everyone clapped and cheered. Then the other fairies swished
their wands, too. Soon, it was a huge firework show fit for a fairysaur.
"Thank you, everyone!" called Flyss. "This is the best present, ever."

# Ghoul School

Leo was late for school, again. **"You can still catch the bus if you're quick,"** said Dad, opening the door and pointing outside.

So, Leo grabbed his bag, then raced off as quickly as he could. **"Bye!"** he called, munching on his half-eaten breakfast.

He ran beside the bus, waving his arms, until it stopped. **"Phew,"** said Leo, when the doors opened. But when he sat down, none of his friends were there. The bus was full of **ghosts** instead!

**"Where are we going?"** asked Leo. **"Ghoul School, of course!"** said Tabby, the little girl ghost next to him.

Mr Boo was so excited to welcome a new student to his class. **"Who wants to show Leo some of our best ghost tricks?"** he asked.

So, Leo spent the morning jumping out from behind doors and learning how to walk through walls, just like a real ghost.

Then, the whole class gathered round Mr Boo and he told them the **spookiest** ghost story ever.

When the bell rang at 12pm, Leo opened his lunchbox and took a bite of his sandwich. Instead of eating their own lunch, all his new friends stared. **"We've never seen anyone eat before,"** said Freddie.

That afternoon, the ghosts hurried outside in their sports kits. When Mr Boo blew his whistle, they all flew into the air as Leo watched from below. **"Leo, close your eyes and say, 'I'm not scared,'"** said Mr Boo.

Before he knew it, Leo was flying through the air playing ghost ball, too!

At the end of the day, Leo got back on the bus with his friends.
They played games and sang songs together all the way home.
**"Please come and visit me at my school,"** said Leo, as he waved goodbye.
**"There's nobody I'd rather spend the day with than all of you."**

# Hairy Fairy

Whenever Nyssa fluttered around Fairyland, all she wanted was to be just like the other fairies. **"Morning, Callie!"** she called, wishing she could have beautiful *flowing* hair, too. **"Hi, Frankie,"** she said, wishing she had the same pretty **green** eyes. **"Nice to see you, Trixie,"** she said, wishing she was **tall**, like her.

That night, as Nyssa closed her eyes, she whispered,
**"I hope my wishes finally come true."** Then she fell fast asleep,
dreaming of all the things she wanted to have.

Sure enough, when Nyssa woke up in the morning, something felt different.
Her toes were cold and she was very uncomfortable.

Nyssa realised it was because her bed was too small.
**"Have I grown taller overnight?"** she said.

Then, when she looked in the mirror, Nyssa couldn't believe
it when she saw her beautiful flowing hair and pretty green eyes.
**"My wishes did come true!"** she yelled in delight.

She flew straight into Fairy Square to show off her new looks.
Nyssa loved how her long hair **swished** and **swayed** in the breeze,
but she didn't realise that it hadn't stopped growing since that morning.

It dragged on the ground and the
birds tweeted as they settled inside it.

Then, instead of admiring her pretty new green eyes, all of Nyssa's friends quickly looked away. Frankie even put on her sunglasses!

**"Nyssa, why are your eyes so bright?"** she asked, as she squinted in the light.

Suddenly, Nyssa felt a strange **RUMBLE**.
It wasn't just her hair that had kept growing,
Nyssa was still growing, as well!
Before she knew it, she was towering
high above the toadstool houses.

"**Why are you so tall, Nyssa?**" shouted Trixie up into the clouds.
"**I wished that I was taller... like you,**" called back Nyssa,
who suddenly felt much smaller than she looked.

The fairies flew into the
sky to see their friend.
**"Why did you want to change?"**
asked Frankie.

"We can't play together
if your eyes are too bright to
look at and you're taller than
our houses," said Trixie.

"We like you just the way
you are," said Callie.

26

Nyssa smiled. "**I wish I hadn't ever made any of those silly wishes**,"
she said. With a FLASH and a POP, Nyssa shrunk back to her normal size,
and everything returned to normal.

# POOOOF!

From then on, she promised she
would never wish to be like anyone... except herself!

# Giants Can't Juggle

The Magical Circus was the best show in town. People came from all around to see Una the unicorn ride around the ring on her magical unicycle, the fairies swing on the trapeze and Donnie the dragon balance on the tightrope. **"Woo-hoo!"** called the crowd each night, as they cheered for the performers.

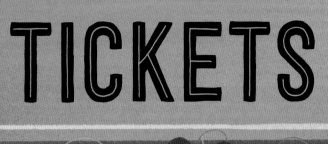

# TICKETS

But poor Humphrey the giant couldn't join in.
He was just too **big** to fit inside the tent! So, instead,
he stayed outside every evening taking tickets. He never
told anyone, but every time he heard the audience roar,
he *dreamed* of being part of the show with his friends.

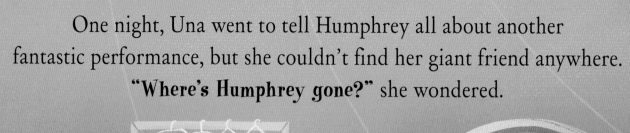

One night, Una went to tell Humphrey all about another fantastic performance, but she couldn't find her giant friend anywhere. **"Where's Humphrey gone?"** she wondered.

Una started looking for clues and, suddenly, she spotted a **huge** chest, which she knew must be Humphrey's. When she peered inside, she gasped.

The chest was full of the most **amazing** circus costumes Una had ever seen. There were spotty outfits, stripy outfits, frilly outfits and feathery outfits.

There were even costumes that were so sparkly they would light up the whole tent! And clever Humphrey had made them all himself.

"Everyone is going to look great performing in these. I can't wait to tell Humphrey when he gets back," said Una. Just then, she heard a THUD, THUD, THUD getting further and further away from the tent.

So, Una looked into the distance... Humphrey was leaving the circus!

32

"Quick, everyone!" she called, rushing back into the tent.
"We've got to stop Humphrey." So, the fairies fluttered and Donnie
flapped and Una flew towards their giant friend as fast as they all could.

"Humphrey, STOOOOP!"
they called together, just as
he was about to leave.

33

Humphrey sniffed and a giant tear rolled down his cheek.
**"If I can't perform with all my friends,
I'm going to leave the circus for good,"** he said.

Una and the others had no idea
Humphrey had felt so left out, and
they knew something had to change.

"I found your amazing costumes," said Una.
"Please come back with us, and we'll all perform in them... together!"

# TICKETS

So, Humphrey's friends invited everyone in town to come and watch a special new performance the very next evening.

"Roll up, roll up," said Una, "for the biggest show ever!"

With that, she led the confused-looking crowd all the way through the circus tent... and then back out to the other side!

There, Humphrey was waiting, dressed in his best costume yet, and he was ready to perform with all of his friends. Everybody clapped and cheered when they saw him.

"**Woo-hoo!**" they shouted, when Humphrey balanced
Una on his head, as she rode on her unicycle.

"**Again, again!**" they called,
when he juggled Donnie and
the fairies, while balancing
on one leg.

Humphrey took a great big bow
in front of his huge audience.
Hooray for Humphrey,
the giant circus clown!

37

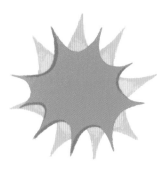 

# Super Squabbles

Dynamite Dylan and Rocket Rosie were the **FASTEST** superheroes in town, but they **squabbled** over everything. **"I can get to the supermarket and back before you can,"** boasted Rosie. So, she zoomed off and zipped up and down the aisles, leaving a trail of fruit and vegetables on the floor behind her.

"Well, I can clean every single window on all the skyscrapers faster than you can," bragged Dylan. He raced high into the sky with ten buckets full of soapy water, but he slopped it all over everyone below.

"OI... HEY... STOP THAT!" the angry people shouted.

39

One very windy day, Farmer Phyllis really needed Dylan and Rosie's help, but they still didn't stop arguing. The farmer pointed to a tree that had blown onto her barn. **"We're going to lose all of our grain!"** she cried.

"I'll save the day," said Dylan.

"Not before I do," insisted Rosie.

The speedy superheroes dashed towards the barn, chasing each other all the way. Rosie got there first, but Dylan found some planks to cover up the hole with. **"I need that!"** called Rosie, and they raced around and around in circles until suddenly, they stopped.

They were tied together with their capes! **"I'm stuck,"** muttered Dylan. **"So am I,"** mumbled Rosie. Then they saw how worried Farmer Phyllis and the farm animals looked, and they knew what they had to do.

**"You wiggle this way,"** said Rosie...

... **"and I'll shuffle that way,"** said Dylan.

In no time at all, they were free,
and they set off in different directions.
As quick as a flash, the barn was fixed
and the farmer's grain was safe.

"Thank you, Rosie and Dylan," she said.
"We knew we could count on the best
superhero team in town!"

# Teenycorn to the Rescue

Everyone in the castle used to love hearing Nina's exciting stories, for she was the bravest knight in the kingdom! But they soon grew tired of her tales when she started **boasting** about the strange beasts she'd defeated single-handedly.

In fact, Nina had become more **big-headed** with every adventure.

**"The monster had 15 arms,"** Nina told the cooks.
**"And I defeated him all by myself!"**
It was the same when she told the maids about the
magical talking lion with three heads and when she bragged to
the prince and princess about the trolls riding on ghostly serpents.

One day, the trumpets sounded loudly.

TOOT-TOOOOT!

There were whispers around the kingdom that a giant was approaching, and he needed to be stopped before he destroyed the castle.
**"I'll defeat him,"** said Nina, marching down to the stables.
**"Get my horse ready and I'll be on my way!"**

But Nina's horse, Hero, was too tired from their adventures to go anywhere. **"Bring me the next best stallion in the stables,"** demanded Nina.

The stable workers looked nervous. The other horses were preparing for battle in case the giant arrived. So, when they brought out Hero's replacement, Nina was furious.

It was a tiny baby unicorn with sparkly fur and a rainbow mane.
**"This is...err... Teeny,"** one of the stable boys said under his breath.

**"I can't ride THAT!"** yelled Nina,
her cheeks turning bright red.
But just then there was a loud...

# THUD, THUD!

Nina sighed. She had no choice but to fly with Teeny towards the deep, dark forest.

When they arrived, there were shadows all around. Nina shivered, and suddenly she heard a **CRACK!** The brave knight jumped up and ran away, because what no one else knew was that... she wasn't really brave at all!

Hero had defeated every single beast, while Nina pretended it was her. Now that he wasn't here, she'd left poor little Teeny all alone.

A few minutes later, Nina peeked out from the bushes she was hiding in and whispered, **"Teeny, where are you?"** But Teeny was nowhere to be seen. Then there was a **BOOM, BOOM!** Nina was about to dive back into the bushes when she saw a burst of magical sparkles.

Teeny was fighting the giant!
The brave little unicorn flew around and
around the giant's head until he got so dizzy
that he toppled over into a pile of leaves.

They returned to the castle and everybody cheered.
**"The giant is gone! The giant is gone!"**

Nina was just about to start boasting all about it as usual,
but this time she stopped. After how she'd treated Teeny,
she knew she had to tell the truth.

"Teeny is the real hero. She was much braver than I was," she said. Then Nina told them everything, even the real reason Hero was so tired. Everyone agreed it was the bravest thing Nina had ever done, and she promised never to boast again!

# The Missing Horn

It was a beautiful day in Unicorn Land, and Twinkle and her friends were playing high above the clouds. **"You can't catch ME!"** called Honeydew, as she chased a dancing sunbeam.

**"No, I'M the fastest,"** laughed Marshmallow, sliding down a rainbow.

**"Wait for me!"** called Twinkle.

54

Usually, Twinkle **ZOOMED** far ahead of the others, but today her wings felt heavy and she couldn't keep up. Soon, Twinkle fell even further behind her friends, and then she realised that she was floating down to the ground. She flapped as hard as she could, but her magic wasn't working!

Twinkle floated down and down until she landed with a soft **BUMP**.
**"Where am I?"** she whispered, looking all around her.

Everything was covered in a white blanket and the
ground crunched beneath her. She and her friends must have
been playing much further away from home than she thought.

Then, Twinkle caught sight of her reflection in an icy lake. "Oh, no!" she gasped. No wonder her magic wasn't working... her horn had completely disappeared! **"If I don't find a new one by the end of the day, I'll turn into a normal pony and lose all my powers for good."**

"**Don't worry,**" said a kind voice, as Twinkle began to cry.
When she turned around, she saw a snowman smiling at her.
She explained everything and told him why she needed a new horn.

"**And if I don't get my magic back,
I won't be able to fly home,**" sniffed Twinkle.

"I can help you find a new horn in no time!" he yelled.
At Mrs Chill's Ice Creams they ordered a
Bubblegum Surprise in an extra-large cone.

"**There!**" said Snowman, sticking the ice cream on Twinkle's head.
But it quickly slid off and fell onto the floor with a **PLOP!**

Penguin gave Snowman and Twinkle one of his **sparkliest** party hats to use as a new horn...

... but it got tangled in Twinkle's mane and kept slipping over her eyes.

Next, Snowman took Twinkle to visit his friend, Narwhal.
**"Your tusk is amazing. It's just like a horn!"** said Twinkle.

Narwhal took them to an enchanted cave where they found the most beautiful icicles. But of course, they began to melt before they could turn one into a new horn for Twinkle. **"I'm sure there's something else we can try,"** said Snowman, but then, the sun started to go down.

"It's too late," said Twinkle, seeing her reflection in the water. "But even though I can't go home, and I'm going to be a normal pony without any magic, I'm so pleased that I've made a new friend like you."

Snowman felt warm and happy inside.
Then, he saw his own reflection.

**"It's not too late!"** he called, jumping up in the air.
He grabbed his carrot nose and placed it on Twinkle's forehead.

She began to **glow** from head to toe, and as Twinkle spread her wings,
she knew her friend's kindness had brought back her magic.

"**Thank you so much, Snowman,**" she said. With a new horn and her
magic restored, she could return to Unicorn Land where she truly belonged.
But first, with a shake of her mane, Twinkle gave Snowman a new nose.
"**Now you can remember our adventures together forever,**" she said.

Before she left, there was just time for one last adventure. So, they soared into the clouds with a **WHOOSH!** They raced past the stars and whizzed around the moon.

"I'll never forget you," said Twinkle, placing Snowman back on the ground. "You're the best friend I've ever had."

# Twirl Like a Yeti

Jamie loved to dance. His bedroom walls were covered with posters of famous dancers and he jumped, leaped and twirled around all day, pretending he was on a real stage.

One day, he noticed his sister putting a tutu into her gym bag. She was going to ballet class!

"I'll come, too!" he said.

"But boys don't do ballet," said Lizzie. Jamie stared out into the garden, feeling sad. Then, he saw a flash of fuzzy purple through the window.

"What was that?" he thought. When Jamie crept downstairs and peered outside, he couldn't believe his eyes.

There, in his very own back garden, was a yeti... and he was spinning and twirling around exactly like Jamie did in his bedroom!

The yeti moved so gracefully that Jamie couldn't help but start clapping. The fuzzy purple yeti was so startled, he fell into a rosebush mid-leap.

"**Thank you,**" he said, standing up and taking a bow.
"**Do you like dancing, too?**" Jamie nodded and told
the yeti all about his sister's ballet class.

"None of the other yetis like to dance either,
but I love it so much that I do it anyway,
anywhere I can!" he said.

Jamie finally understood. It didn't matter if he was the only boy in his sister's class! He loved ballet, so he was going to go.

He spent the whole afternoon twirling around the garden with the yeti, until the moon came out and shone down on them like a spotlight.

The next day, Jamie arrived at ballet class before his sister.
**"What are you doing here?"** she asked, when she saw
him practising in front of the mirror.

**"I'm ready to twirl like a yeti!"**
said Jamie, as he leaped into the air!

# Unicorn Races

It was race day in Unicorn Land and all the competitors were ready to begin. Speedicorn won the race every year, but the others had all been training really hard to see if they could beat her this time.

Soon, it was time for the fairy queen to announce the start.

She fluttered into the air and called, **"Three... two... one... GO!"**
With a swish of her wand, the unicorns flapped their wings,
kicked off from the ground and whooshed into the sky.

The crowd waved their flags and cheered,
as the unicorns whizzed past the twinkling
stars and galloped over the moon.

Speedicorn glided all the way through Candy Land in first place, and she flew over every candy-cane hurdle before the others had even reached Marshmallow Mountain.

Babycorn was following closely behind, when suddenly, he stopped on Syrup Street. **"Oh, no!"** he called. **"I'm stuck!"** Babycorn couldn't move, no matter how hard he tried.

Then, Friendlicorn stopped to help. **"You just need a sprinkle of sugar from the gumdrop tree,"** she said, and soon they were on their way.

SYRUP STREET

As Babycorn waved to the mermaids at the Enchanted Waterfall, he saw Speedicorn in the distance. **"Maybe I can catch her after all,"** he thought.

Babycorn flapped his wings extra hard, and by the time he reached Rainbow Park, he was in second place. **"You can do it!"** he heard Friendlicorn shout.

Babycorn bounced from cloud to cloud, getting closer to Speedicorn each time.

**BOING!**

**BOING!**

Finally, he jumped onto the rainbow slide.

There was Speedicorn, and she was about to shoot down the slide, too!
"**WHEEEE!**" yelled Babycorn, as he twisted and turned all the way
to the end with Speedicorn beside him.

FINISH

At the bottom, he finally zoomed past her, and crossed the finish line.
"**Well done, Babycorn,**" said Speedicorn. "**You're a real winner!**"

# Playtime Potion

Elly and Priya were playing fairies with Priya's pet frog, Sparkles. They collected lots of pretty petals from all around the garden and put them all in Priya's fairy bucket. Then they mixed their special fairy potion together with a whoosh of water from the garden hose.

"**It just needs a touch of fairy dust,**" said Elly,
sprinkling some pink blossoms into the bucket. **RIBBIT!** went Sparkles.
The girls closed their eyes and whispered some magic words, and then
they swished their wands over the top of their fairy potion.

Suddenly, there was a
**ZAP** and a POOF...

When Elly and Priya opened their eyes, everything in the garden looked different.

They looked up at the flowers towering high above their heads, and even creepy-crawlies seemed **huge**. **"Your potion worked,"** said a voice. It was coming from Sparkles the frog. He could talk!

**"Look at your fairy wings,"** said Priya. **"They're real!"**
When the two friends finally fluttered over to the garden pond
to look at their reflection, they saw they had both shrunk down
to the size of tiny magical fairies.

They twirled around in delight and swished
their wands until magical sparks flew everywhere.

"That's just the start," said Sparkles. "Come with me!"
So Priya and Elly followed the magical frog past the shed,
beyond the vegetable patch and through some hedges,
right down to the bottom of the garden.

There, among the flowers, was a tree
surrounded by spotty toadstools.

"**Tap your wands three times and see what happens**," said Sparkles.
So, the girls did just that.

TAP...

TAP...

TAP!

Sure enough, a tiny fairy door opened.
"**Hello, Sparkles**," said a cheerful fairy inside,
whose name was Jovi. "**This must be Priya and Elly!**"

Jovi showed them around her tree-trunk home and introduced Elly and Priya to all the other garden fairies. **"Would you like to stay for tea?"** she asked. As soon as the girls had nodded their heads, a magical feast appeared on plates that floated in the air.

**"How did you discover the secret to the magic fairy potion?"** asked Jovi's friend, Ivy, through a mouthful of marshmallow surprise.

"We just knew we needed to add fairy dust," said Elly.
The garden fairies asked them never to tell anyone,
so it would stay a secret forever. "We promise," said Elly and Priya.

85

As the sun went down, it was time to go home.
**"The magic will wear off soon,"** said Jovi.
She waved goodbye to her new friends as
they **fluttered** into the distance.

Then, by the time the stars
were twinkling in the sky,
Elly and Priya were back
to their normal sizes.

"**What a magical adventure,**" said Elly, and she took off her fairy wings that were just pretend again. "**I can't wait to play fairies again tomorrow.**"

"**Thanks for everything, Sparkles,**" said Priya.
But instead of replying, he just winked back at them. **RIBBIT!**

# The Magical Moon Boat

Benji and Lily had always wanted to meet a real-life mermaid. They loved reading about them in books and dreamed of seeing one whenever they went swimming in the sea. One day, Benji had an idea. **"Maybe there are mermaids in the river,"** he said to his sister.

They couldn't wait to see if they were right,
and they got their chance when they went camping that weekend.

**"This looks like a good place for mermaid spotting,"** said Dad, and they
munched on a picnic of cheese sandwiches and sticky strawberry shortcake.
**"I wonder what mermaids like to eat,"** said Lily.

They soon couldn't resist running into the water and paddling by the bank.

SPLISH.

SPLOSH,

SPLASH!

Suddenly, they heard Dad calling from the other side of the river. He pulled back the tall reeds and there was a rowing boat bobbing in the water. **"We're going on an adventure,"** he said. **"Grab an oar!"**

Lily and Benji climbed into the boat.
They were sure they'd spot a mermaid if they could explore the whole river!

So, they spent the afternoon rowing up and down. They saw croaking frogs,
quacking ducks and gurgling fish, but there were no mermaids anywhere.
Then, the sun started to go down.

"We'd better get back to the tent before it gets dark," said Dad.
Benji and Lily were disappointed. "I wish we'd seen a mermaid," said Lily.
Just then, the moon came out and the stars began to shine,
and suddenly, something strange happened.

"We're rowing underwater!"
called Benji.

And they were! Seaweed was swaying all around them and fish darted in between the rocks. Dad kept rowing. **"But why aren't we sinking?"** asked Lily.

**"It's magic!"** said a voice. They turned around and there, before their very eyes, was a real-life mermaid, just like they'd always dreamed!

They followed the mermaid, whose name was Silky, in their rowing boat all the way to her magical underwater home on the riverbed. Everything twinkled and shone under the moonlight.

"Come and meet my friends," said Silky, when they arrived. "This is Echo and Nori."

"Would you like a seaweed sandwich?" asked Nori.
"So, this is what mermaids eat," Lily whispered to Benji,
who was munching pebble popcorn.

They stayed for a whole mermaid midnight feast,
complete with delicious bubble pie. And when everybody was full,
they listened to Silky, Nori and Echo singing lullabies until it was time to go.

As they all climbed back into their rowing boat and waved goodbye, Silky swam over and placed glowing necklaces over Benji and Lily's heads.

"Any time you want to visit, just close your eyes and make a wish," she said. Lily and Benji couldn't wait for their next river adventure!